EARLY BIRD STORIES™

# Fall Harvest Fun

Martha E. H. Rustad

Illustrated by Amanda Enright

LERNER PUBLICATIONS ◆ MINNEAPOLIS

# NOTE TO EDUCATORS

Find text recall questions at the end of each chapter. Critical-thinking and text feature questions are available on page 23. These help young readers learn to think critically about the topic by using the text, text features, and illustrations.



Lerner Publications Company
A division of Lerner Publishing Group, Inc.
241 First Avenue North
Minneapolis, MN 55401 USA

For reading levels and more information, look up this title at www.lernerbooks.com.

Photos on page 22 are used with the permission of: Denis Pogostin/Shutterstock.com (planting), LianeM/Shutterstock.com (weeding); @erics/Shutterstock.com (apples).

Main body text set in Billy Infant 22/28.
Typeface provided by SparkyType.

**Library of Congress Cataloging-in-Publication Data**

Names: Rustad, Martha E. H. (Martha Elizabeth Hillman), 1975- author. | Enright, Amanda, illustrator.
Title: Fall harvest fun / Martha E. H. Rustad ; illustrated by Amanda Enright.
Description: Minneapolis : Lerner Publications, [2018] | Series: Fall fun | Includes bibliographical references and index.
Identifiers: LCCN 2017050327 (print) | LCCN 2017055562 (ebook) | ISBN 9781541524927 (eb pdf) | ISBN 9781541520028 (lb : alk. paper) | ISBN 9781541527195 (pb : alk. paper)
Subjects: LCSH: Food crops—Harvesting—Juvenile literature. | Harvesting—Juvenile literature. | Harvest festivals—Juvenile literature. | Autumn—Juvenile literature.
Classification: LCC SB129 (ebook) | LCC SB129 .R924 2018 (print) | DDC 631.5/5—dc23

LC record available at https://lccn.loc.gov/2017050327

Manufactured in the United States of America
1-44338-34584-1/11/2018

# TABLE OF CONTENTS

CHAPTER 1

# FALL FOODS

**Yum!** I help my dad make applesauce. We picked the apples right off the tree.

Some of my favorite foods are harvested in fall.
But last spring, they started off small.

**When are many foods harvested?**

CHAPTER 2

# GROWING FOOD

Spring is for planting.
In spring, farmers plant seeds.

Tiny plants push out of the dirt.
They will grow into pumpkins, potatoes, and corn.
In orchards, trees blossom in the spring.

Summer is for growing.

Leaves turn sunlight into food for growing plants.

Roots gather water for thirsty plants.

Slowly, plants change and grow.

Weeds can crowd out growing plants.
Bugs eat growing leaves.

Farmers and gardeners work hard to stop weeds and bugs.

How do roots help plants?

CHAPTER 3

# HARVESTING FOOD

Fall is for harvesting.
Plants stop growing in the cool fall weather.

Food is ready for harvest.

Farmers harvest fruit from orchard trees in fall. People pick apples and peaches by hand.

Pecans fall from pecan trees. Farmers sometimes use machines to shake pecans from trees.

How do people harvest apples?

CHAPTER 4

# HARVEST FESTIVALS

People around the world have festivals in fall. They celebrate all the food harvested that year.

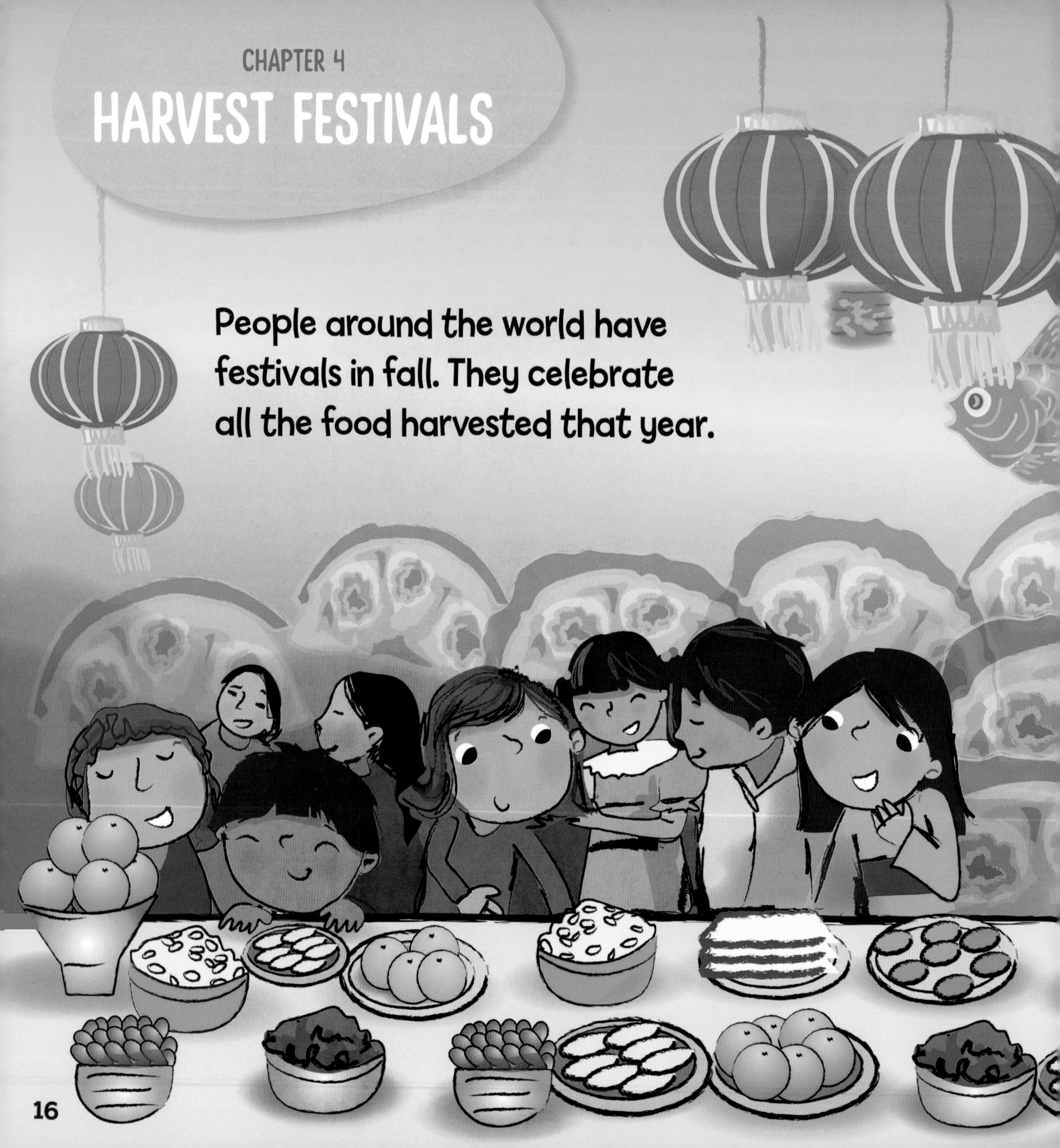

In Korea, people have the Harvest Moon Festival. They eat rice cakes and play games.

At the Yam Festival in Ghana, people eat yams, have parades, and make music.

In North America, families celebrate Thanksgiving. They eat big meals and spend time together.

In fall, the earth gets ready to rest.
Farmers and gardeners get ready to rest too.

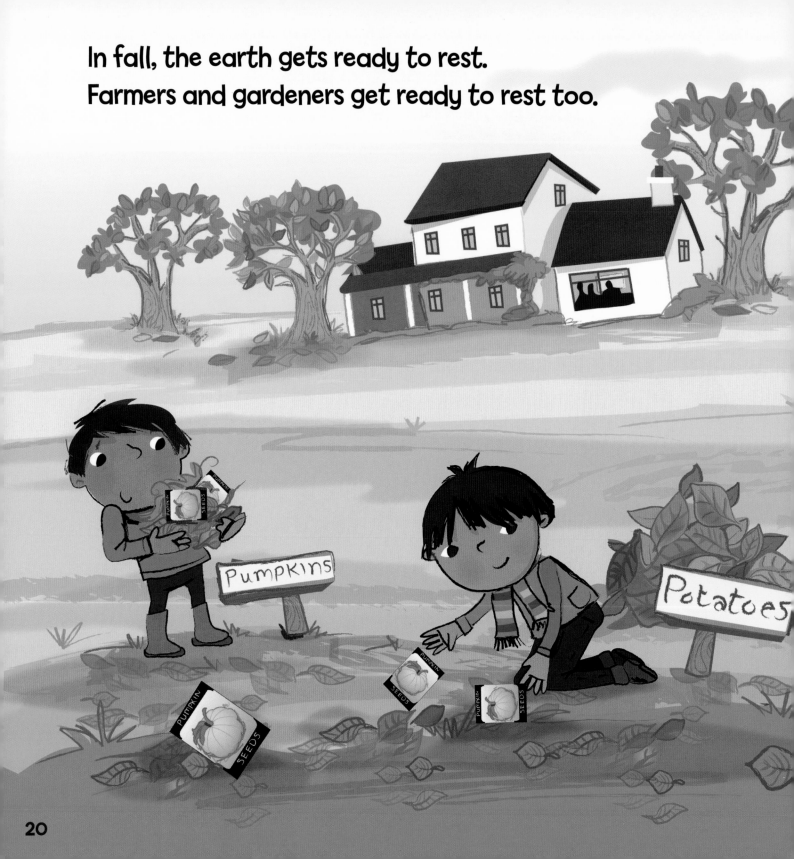

What fall foods would you like to celebrate?

Why do people have festivals in fall?

# LEARN ABOUT FALL

Farmers and gardeners plant seeds far apart. Plants need lots of room to grow. By fall, the plants will fill the spaces.

The green color inside leaves is called chlorophyll. Chlorophyll makes food for plants.

People pull weeds with tools, machines, and their hands.

Some farmers plant grain seeds in fall. These grains grow a little in fall. They stop growing in winter. They start growing again in spring. They are ready in early summer.

Farmers know when apples and peaches are ready to be picked. The fruit is easy to pull off the tree.

# THINK ABOUT FALL:
## CRITICAL-THINKING AND TEXT FEATURE QUESTIONS

**What food is harvested in fall where you live?**

**Why do you think farmers harvest food when the weather turns colder?**

**What is chapter 4 in this book called?**

**Can you find all the pages in the book that show pumpkins?**

LERNER SOURCE™

Expand learning beyond the printed book. Download free, complementary educational resources for this book from our website, www.lerneresource.com.

# GLOSSARY

**blossom:** when flowers grow on a tree or a bush

**celebrate:** to do something fun, such as have a party, on a special day

**harvest:** to gather plants. Food is harvested when it is ready to be eaten.

**pecan:** a nut that grows on trees

**root:** a part of a plant that grows underground. Roots soak up water for the plant.

# TO LEARN MORE

## BOOKS

**Lindeen, Mary.** ***I Watch Fall Harvests.*** Minneapolis: Lerner Publications, 2017. Learn more about the food that farmers harvest in fall.

**Schuh, Mari.** ***Harvest in Fall.*** Minneapolis: Jump!, 2014. Find out how farmers harvest food and how it gets to stores for people to eat.

## WEBSITE

**Activity Village: Harvest Festival**
https://www.activityvillage.co.uk/harvest-festival
Find crafts, coloring pages, and activities to help you celebrate the harvest.

# INDEX